# PADDINGTON AT THE CIRCUS

For older children Michael Bond has
written nine Paddington story books,
all illustrated by Peggy Fortnum

*CIP data may be found at the end of the book.*

# Paddington
# at the Circus

## MICHAEL BOND AND
## FRED BANBERY

Random House

New York

First American Edition 1974. Text Copyright © 1973 by Michael Bond.
Illustrations Copyright © 1973 by Fred Banbery.
All rights reserved under International and Pan-American Copyright Conventions.
Published in the United States by Random House, Inc., New York.
Originally published in Great Britain by William Collins Sons & Co., Ltd., London.
*Manufactured in the United States of America*   1  2  3  4  5  6  7  8  9  0

One day Paddington was out doing his morning
shopping when he came across a very strange-
looking man pasting a picture on a wall.

It showed a huge tent decorated with red and
green and blue lights and streamers, and across
the middle were the words—THE GREATEST
SHOW ON EARTH! ONE NIGHT ONLY.
BOOK NOW.

When Paddington got home he hurried
indoors to tell the others.

"The Greatest Show on Earth?" repeated
Jonathan, giving Judy a wink. "In a *tent*? You

must have been dreaming!"

Then Judy announced the good news. It was a circus and they all had tickets for the front row that very evening.

Paddington had never been to a circus before and he grew more and more excited as the time drew near.

The lights were already on when they arrived and there was a lovely smell of sawdust in the air. It looked very gay and inviting.

But the circus itself was even more exciting. There was a band, and a ringmaster in a top hat, and even a lady selling ice-cream cones.

Altogether there was so much to see Paddington didn't know what to look at first.

"I think I would like to join a circus, Mr. Brown," he announced happily.

Then he caught sight of the man he had met that morning. He was in the middle of the ring, balancing a bucket on the end of a long pole. "That's a clown," explained Judy. "He's standing on stilts. That's why he looks so tall."

Paddington waved
and the man came over
and bent down to shake
his paw. The bucket
tipped, and Paddington
jumped up in alarm.

Luckily the bucket was empty and it was tied to the end of the pole, so Paddington soon got over his fright.

Mr. Brown bought him an ice-cream cone and as the band started to play they sat back to enjoy the show. All, that is, except Paddington.

15

The first act was barely over when he had
yet another shock. Looking up toward the roof
of the tent, he saw a man hanging from a rope.

"I expect that's one of the Popular Prices,"
began Jonathan, looking at the program.
"They are trapeze artists . . ."

But Paddington didn't stop to listen. "Don't worry, Mr. Price," he called. "I'm coming!"

Before the others could stop him, Paddington
was halfway up the nearest tent pole.

He clambered onto a small platform and then

nearly fell off again with surprise when he saw
a second man coming toward him.

He was dressed in tights and was riding a bicycle.

But Paddington was not nearly as surprised as the men themselves.

"Look out!" shouted the leader. "Hold on!"

Paddington did as he was told. He grabbed the nearest thing he could see.

The next moment he found himself flying
through the air.

The audience had been clapping before, but when Paddington appeared they clapped more loudly than ever, for they all thought he was part of the act.

He missed the platform on the other side and
began to swing backward and forward, getting
lower and lower, until he came to a stop over
the middle of the ring.

"Don't let go!" shouted the ringmaster. "Whatever you do—don't let go!"

And then he stopped and a look of horror came over his face as something soft and white landed on his beautifully brushed top hat.

"Crikey!" exclaimed Jonathan. "Paddington's ice cream!"

In the end it was Paddington's
friend, the clown, who saved him.
He held up the bucket on the
end of his pole so that Paddington
could step into it.

The cheers as Paddington landed in the ring made the whole tent shake.

"Best act I've seen in years!" shouted a man near the Browns. "More! More!"

Paddington gave the man a hard stare as he stepped out of the bucket.

He'd had quite enough of being a trapeze artist for one night.

Even the ringmaster had to admit that
Paddington had been the star act of the
evening, and at the end of the show he gave him
another ice-cream cone and insisted he take part in
the Grand Parade.

"It's a pity we're only here for one night," he
said sadly. "I'd like to have you in my circus all
the time."

"Do you still want to join a circus, Paddington?" asked Judy, later that night.

Paddington shook his head. And then a faraway look came into his eyes as he tested his sheets carefully to make sure he was safely tucked in.

"But it was *very* nice to be asked," he said. "I don't suppose there are many bears from Peru who can say they've been on a trapeze!"